CAIRN-BRIDGE SCHOOL
CAIRN-BRIDGE
INVERNESS-SHIRE
PH23 3AF

KU-413-269

play forever on video and

© Disney

This is a Parragon book
First published in 2006
Parragon
Queen Street House
4 Queen Street
Bath, BA1 1HE, UK

ISBN 1-40547-496-3
Printed in China

Walt Disney's

CLASSIC

SLEEPING BEAUTY

p

Long ago, in a far away land, there lived a king and queen who held a great feast to celebrate the birth of their baby daughter, Aurora.

The King of a nearby country, and
his young son, Philip, were guests at
the feast.

The two Kings made plans for Philip
and Aurora to marry on the Princess'
sixteenth birthday.

Also at the celebrations were the Princess' three fairy godmothers — Flora, Fauna and Merryweather. Each of them brought a special gift for the little Princess.

First, Flora waved her magic wand over the baby's cradle and said, "I give you the gift of beauty."

Then, Fauna waved her wand and said, "I give you the gift of song."

Finally, Merryweather fluttered over to the cradle. She raised her wand and…

Suddenly, there was a crack of thunder. Maleficent, the wicked fairy, stormed in. She was furious that she had not been invited to the celebrations.

Stroking her pet raven, Maleficent glared at the baby Princess "I also have a gift for you," she hissed. "Before the sun sets on your sixteenth birthday, you will prick your finger on the spindle of a spinning wheel and die!"

Maleficent threw back her head and laughed wickedly. Then, she disappeared in a cloud of purple smoke.

Merryweather gave a gentle cough.
"I still have my gift for the Princess,"
she reminded the horrified King
and Queen.

She went over to the sleeping baby and whispered, "When the spindle pricks your finger, you will not die. Instead, you will fall into an enchanted sleep. From this slumber you shall wake when true love's kiss the spell shall break."

The King was still worried about his
daughter's safety. He ordered every
spinning wheel in the kingdom to be
burned. Then, he and the Queen
sadly agreed to the fairy godmothers'
plan to protect Aurora until her
sixteenth birthday had passed…

Flora, Fauna and Merryweather
renamed the Princess, Briar Rose.
They took her far away to a little
cottage in the woods. There, the
fairies put away their magic wands.
They disguised themselves as
peasant women so that Maleficent
wouldn't be able to find them.

As the years passed, Maleficent kept searching for the Princess – but she never found her.

As the Princess' sixteenth birthday drew nearer, Maleficent sent her trusted pet raven to try and find her. It was Maleficent's last chance…

The morning of Briar Rose's birthday came. The three fairies sent her to collect berries so they could prepare some birthday surprises.

After gathering the berries, Briar Rose rested in a woodland glade. She sang about falling in love with a handsome prince.

Her friends, the animals and birds, found a cloak, a hat and a pair of boots. They dressed up as a make-believe prince. Briar Rose joined in their game, dancing and singing with them.

The clothes belonged to Prince
Philip, who after a long ride, was
resting in the woods with his horse.

Philip was enchanted by the
beautiful voice coming through the
trees and went to find the singer.

As soon as they met, Briar Rose and the handsome stranger fell in love. They felt sure that they had met before – once upon a dream.

When it was time for Briar Rose to leave, they arranged to meet that evening at the cottage in the woods.

Meanwhile, the three fairies were in a terrible muddle! Fauna had baked a birthday cake. But the mixture was too runny and the cake wouldn't stand up!

Flora and Merryweather had made a special gown for Briar Rose. But it was a *very* funny shape!

"It's no use," said Merryweather.
"We need to use magic to sort this
out. I'll fetch the wands."

Before they dared to use their wands, the fairies blocked up every gap in the cottage. They had to stop any magic dust escaping and alerting Maleficent to their hideaway. But they forgot to block the chimney!

It was so wonderful to be able to use magic again! Flora waved her wand and a beautiful pink gown appeared. Then Merryweather waved her wand and changed the gown to blue. Flora changed it back to pink. All the time, magic dust was escaping from the chimney.

Maleficent's raven was searching nearby. He saw the magic dust and decided to investigate.

By the time Briar Rose returned to the cottage, the presents were all ready. She thanked her fairy godmothers for the beautiful new gown and the delicious cake.

"This is the happiest day of my life," she said.

Then she began to tell them about
the handsome stranger she had met
in the woods. She planned to meet
him that very evening. "It's time we
told Briar Rose the truth," said Fauna.
Up on the chimney, Maleficent's
raven smiled.

So, Briar Rose discovered that she was really a princess and would soon have to marry Prince Philip.

"Today you must return to the palace and start your new life," said Flora.

Briar Rose was heartbroken. She
didn't want to marry a prince. She
had fallen in love with the handsome
stranger she had met in the woods.

By now, the raven had heard enough. He flapped his wings and flew away to tell his mistress that the search for Princess Aurora was finally over.

As soon as darkness fell, the fairy godmothers led Briar Rose through the forest to the palace. They had no idea that Maleficent was already there, lying in wait for them…

At the palace, the fairy godmothers left Aurora in a quiet room to rest. Suddenly, a strange glowing light appeared. Aurora followed it in a trance-like state. It led her up a winding staircase to an attic room. Inside the room was Maleficent – waiting by a spinning wheel.

Maleficent urged the Princess to touch the spinning wheel. Aurora reached out. She pricked her finger on the spindle and fell to the floor.

As soon as the fairy godmothers
found Aurora lying by the spinning
wheel, they cast a sleeping spell
over the entire palace.

Luckily, the fairies had discovered that Prince Philip was the stranger who Briar Rose had fallen in love with. Only his kiss could wake her!

So, while everyone was asleep, the fairies thought of a plan. They would return to the cottage, find Philip and bring him back to the palace.

But they were too late! Maleficent and her soldiers had trapped the Prince at the cottage and had captured him.

Maleficent took Philip back to her castle where she threw him into her deepest dungeon. She fastened him to the wall with heavy chains and left him there to die.

35

When the fairies didn't find Philip at the cottage, they guessed Maleficent may have captured him. They quickly made their way to her castle.

As soon as it was safe, the fairies magically appeared in the dungeon and freed the Prince. They waved their wands and armed him with a magic shield of virtue and a sword of truth.

Then, the Prince galloped off to the
palace to rescue the Princess...

When Maleficent discovered that the Prince had escaped, she roared with rage. She cast a spell and surrounded the palace with a forest of thorns. But Philip was able to cut his way through with his magic sword.

Suddenly, a huge and terrible black
dragon appeared over him. The
dragon laughed wickedly – it was
Maleficent! Philip held up his magic
shield so that the dragon's scorching
flames could not touch him.

The battle had begun! The dragon
soared into the air and swooped
down towards Philip.

The Prince hurled his magic sword at the dragon. The beast crashed to the ground – Maleficent was dead!

Prince Philip raced towards the
palace. He quickly found the room
where the sleeping beauty lay. As he
gently kissed her, she opened her
eyes – the spell was broken!

The fairy godmothers' spell was broken too. All round the palace, people began to wake from their enchanted sleep.

That evening, a magnificent ball was held to celebrate the wedding of Philip and Aurora. The Princess, dressed in the beautiful blue gown, danced happily in the arms of her prince.

As the fairy godmothers watched
over them, Flora couldn't resist
turning the blue gown back to pink.
But Merryweather turned it back to
blue. And so it went on… pink…
blue… pink… blue…

Yours to own on DISNEP DVD

WALT DISNEP
CLASSICS

Magical stories to